This book belongs to
Space Ranger

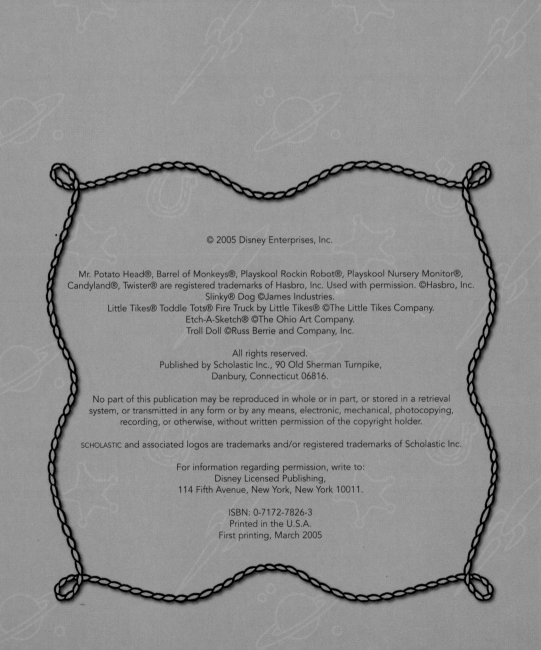

For information regarding permission, write to:
Disney Licensed Publishing,
114 Fifth Avenue, New York, New York 10011.

ISBN: 0-7172-7826-3
Printed in the U.S.A.
First printing, March 2005

DISNEY · PIXAR

TOY STORY

SCHOLASTIC INC.

New York   Toronto   London   Auckland   Sydney
Mexico City   New Delhi   Hong Kong   Buenos Aires

$\int$heriff Woody faced the famous outlaw bank robber Black Bart, as played by Mr. Potato Head.

6

"Reach for the sky, you rascal!" Sheriff Woody said.

Little Andy Davis aimed his two toys at each other. As always, Sheriff Woody won the fight. Andy loved Woody the best of all of his toys.

Just then Andy heard his
mother calling him. It was time
for Andy's birthday party!

When Andy was gone, all his toys could walk and talk.

"Andy's birthday!" Woody said to himself. "This is terrible!"

He ran to Slinky Dog and told him to round up everyone for a meeting.

Woody led the meeting. He reminded the toys about the upcoming move to Andy's new house.

Then Woody added quietly, "And Andy's birthday party has been moved up to today."

The toys panicked!

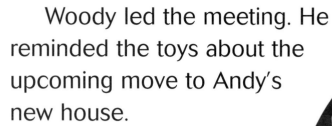

A few toys ran to the window. They saw Andy's friends carrying gifts.

The toys were afraid. What if Andy got new toys? Would he throw away his old ones?

"Don't worry. No one will be thrown away," Woody reassured them.

11

But Woody sent the Green Army Men to watch the party anyway and report back. Luckily, most of the gifts were clothes and games.

Then Andy opened his last present. The soldiers gasped. It was a new toy!

Later, Andy put the new
toy on his bed. After he left,
Woody and the other toys
approached the stranger.

Suddenly the new toy jumped up.
"My name is Buzz Lightyear, and I come to your
planet in peace."

Rex the dinosaur got very excited. "Are you
really here from outer space?"

13

Woody sighed. "Of course not. He's a toy."

"I think the word you're looking for is space ranger," Buzz told him. "I'm captain of the space fleet. As soon as I fix my spaceship, I'll go back home."

All of the toys were impressed, except for Woody.

"I have special wings—I can fly," Buzz told him.

"No, you can't," Woody said.

"Yes, I can. And I can prove it," he said. Then Buzz leapt off the bed. "To infinity and beyond!" he cried.

MAGIC Etch A Sketch SCREEN

16

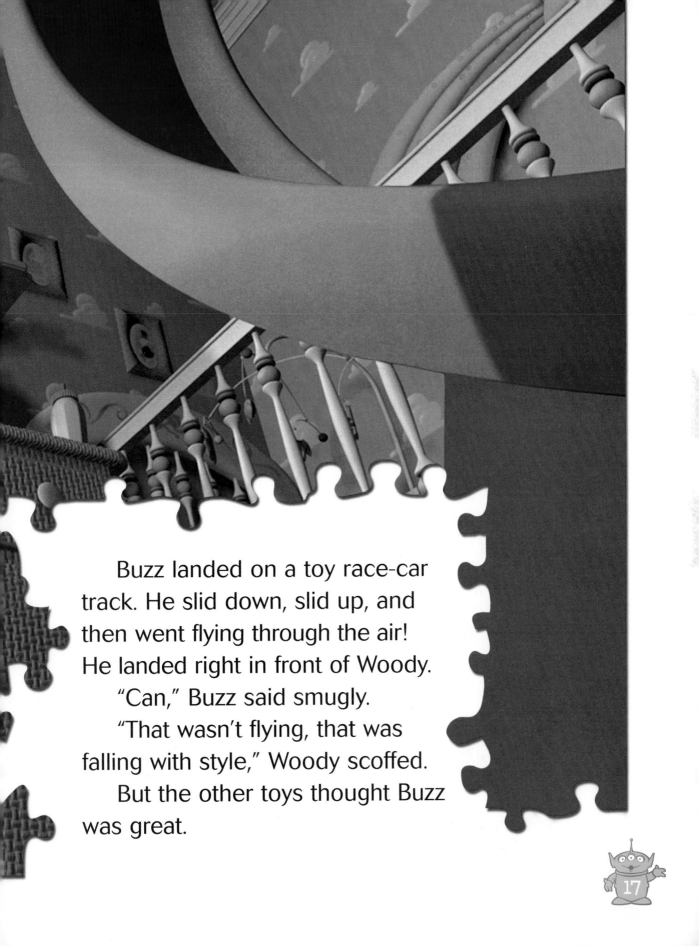

Buzz landed on a toy race-car
track. He slid down, slid up, and
then went flying through the air!
He landed right in front of Woody.

"Can," Buzz said smugly.

"That wasn't flying, that was
falling with style," Woody scoffed.

But the other toys thought Buzz
was great.

17

Suddenly the toys heard shouting. It was Sid, the boy next door. Sid liked to blow up his toys—and that's just what he was doing now! The toys were glad they lived with Andy.

Over the next few days, Andy began to play with Buzz all the time. Woody grew jealous.

One night, Andy was going to Pizza Planet. "You can bring one toy," said his mother.

Woody wanted Andy to bring him, not Buzz. So to make Buzz fall behind the dresser, Woody aimed RC, a remote-controlled car, at Buzz. *ZOOOOM!* Buzz jumped out of the way just in time!

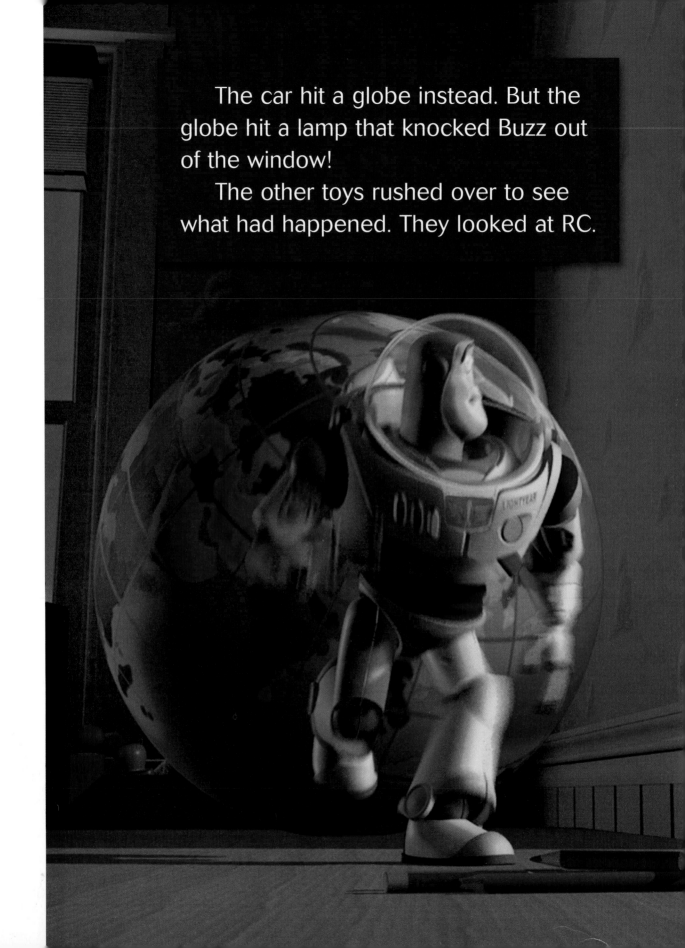

The car hit a globe instead. But the globe hit a lamp that knocked Buzz out of the window!

The other toys rushed over to see what had happened. They looked at RC.

The little car said, *"Whirr, whirr."*

The toys were shocked. They looked at Woody.

"You used RC to knock Buzz out of the window!" Mr. Potato Head accused.

"No!" Woody cried. "I didn't mean to!"

The other toys didn't believe him. Woody didn't know what to say. All the toys were angry with him.

21

Just then Andy came into the room looking for Buzz. Since Andy couldn't find his new toy, he took Woody to the car instead.

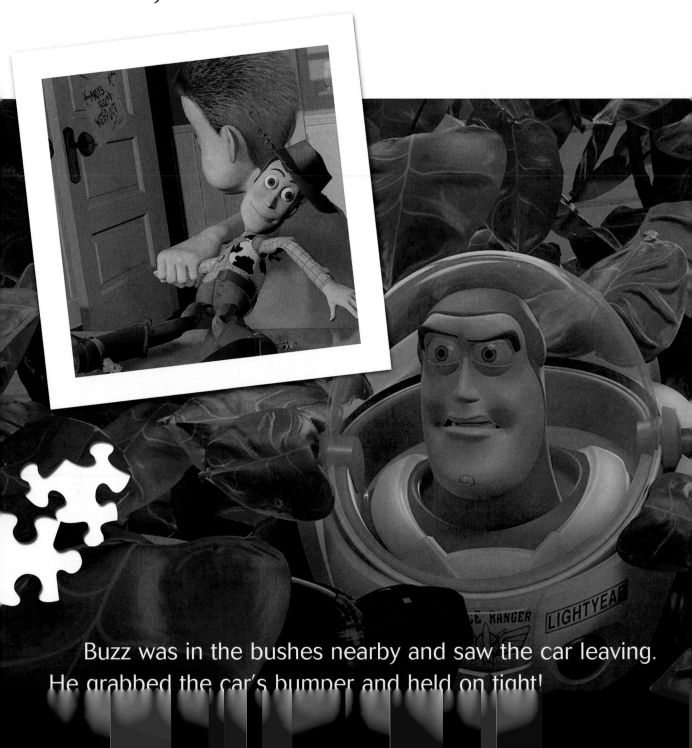

Buzz was in the bushes nearby and saw the car leaving. He grabbed the car's bumper and held on tight!

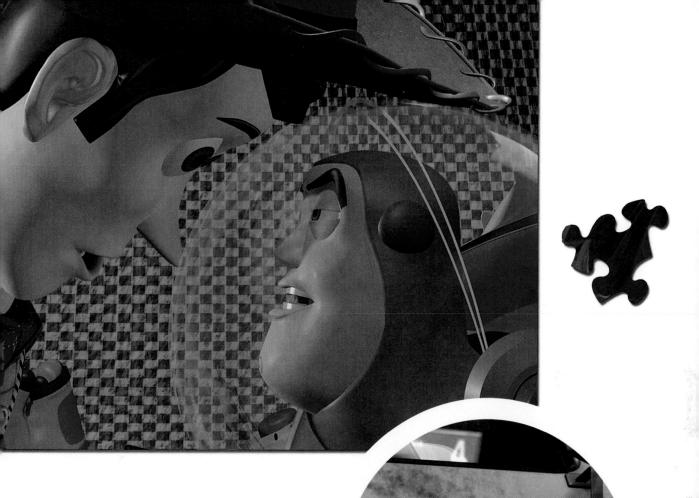

When Andy's mother
stopped for fuel, she and
Andy got out of the car—
and Buzz climbed in.

Woody tried to apologize,
but Buzz didn't believe him.
The two toys began to fight and
rolled out of the open car door. Andy
and his mom left without them! Luckily, Woody noticed
a Pizza Planet van. He and Buzz jumped aboard.

When the toys got to Pizza Planet, they wanted to go inside. But robots guarded the door.

"How are we going to get past the guards?" wondered Woody.

Woody hid inside a big cup. Buzz hid inside a burger box.

They sneaked past the robot guards.

Once they were inside, Woody spotted Andy.

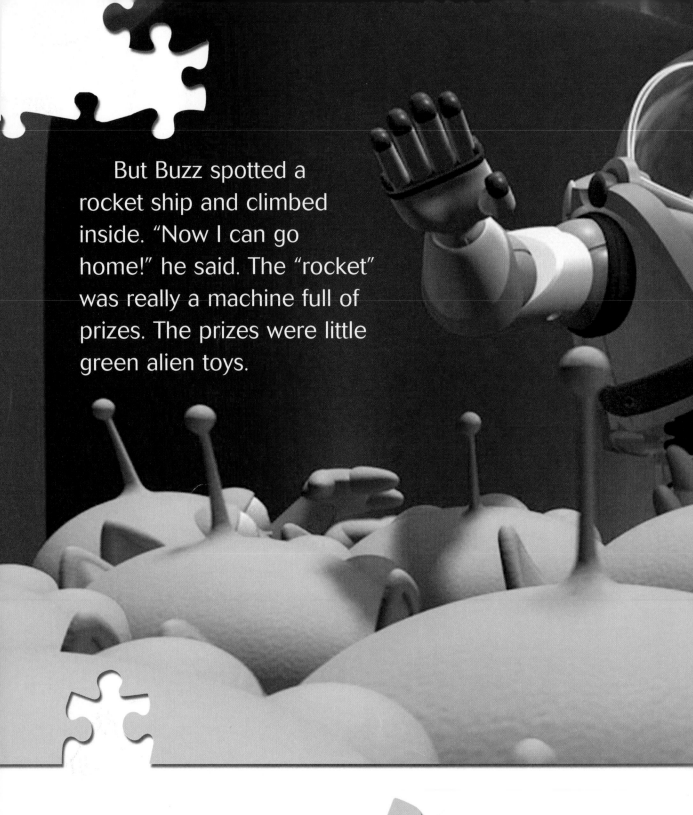

But Buzz spotted a rocket ship and climbed inside. "Now I can go home!" he said. The "rocket" was really a machine full of prizes. The prizes were little green alien toys.

26

Woody knew he had to rescue Buzz.
So he climbed into the rocket, too.

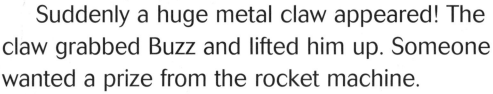 Suddenly a huge metal claw appeared! The claw grabbed Buzz and lifted him up. Someone wanted a prize from the rocket machine.

It was Sid!

Woody tried to save Buzz. Instead, Woody got picked up, too!

Sid laughed a nasty laugh. Now he had two new toys to destroy!

Sid took the toys home to his room. After he left, Woody and Buzz looked around. They saw something moving. Slowly, some strange toys crept out of the darkness.

Woody had never seen anything so horrible.
Sid had ripped apart his toys and put them
back together in weird ways.

The mutant toys moved closer to Woody
and Buzz. Woody and Buzz ran!

They ran to different rooms. Then Buzz saw
something even scarier—a TV commercial for a
Buzz Lightyear toy!

"That can't be right. I'm the real Buzz Lightyear,"
Buzz said to himself. "But what if Woody is right?
What if I am just a toy?"

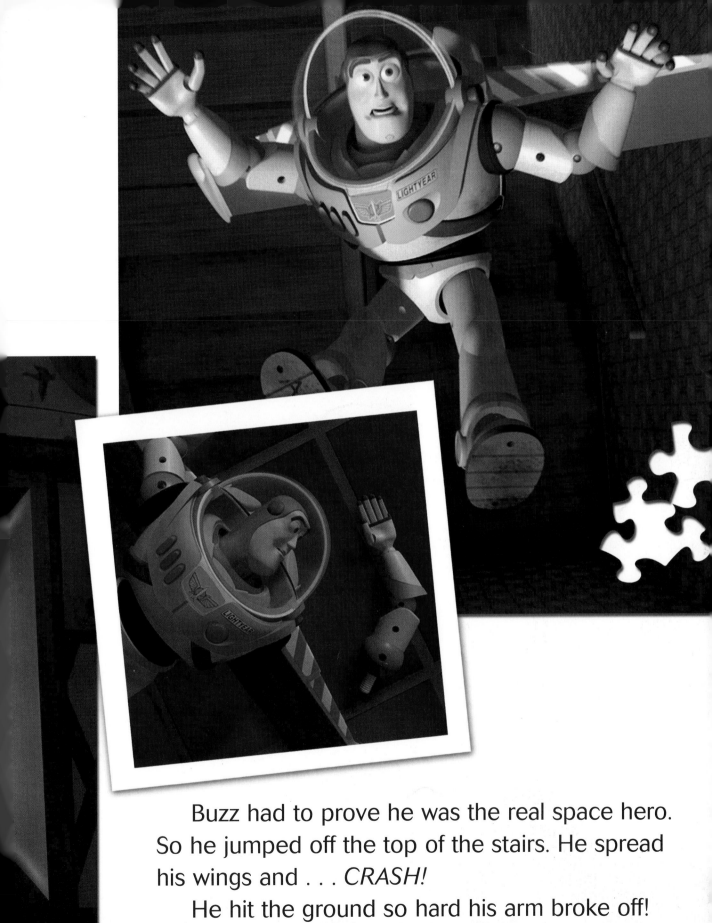

Buzz had to prove he was the real space hero. So he jumped off the top of the stairs. He spread his wings and . . . *CRASH!*

He hit the ground so hard his arm broke off!

Sid's sister found Buzz and brought him to her doll's tea party. Woody sneaked into her room to get Buzz and go home.

"Why bother?" Buzz replied sadly. "I'm just a stupid toy."

As they went back to Sid's room to escape, Woody tried to convince Buzz how important it was to be one of Andy's toys.

Suddenly the mutant toys surrounded Buzz—and fixed his broken arm!

Just then Sid turned up. He taped a rocket to Buzz. He was going to blow him up the next morning!

Woody had to save Buzz. But he couldn't do it alone. He bravely asked the mutant toys for help. They agreed!

The next morning, the
mutant toys followed Woody
to Sid's backyard.
"Reach for the sky!" Woody shouted at Sid.
Sid turned around. He looked at Woody in
shock. How could a toy talk by itself?

"We toys don't like being blown up or ripped apart," Woody told Sid.

The boy gasped. He watched as dozens of toys headed straight for him.

Woody said, "You'd better take good care of your toys. If you don't, we'll find out, Sid!"

Sid screamed and ran. He would never blow up a toy again. Woody and the other toys cheered.

Suddenly Woody saw the moving van in front of Andy's house. He and Buzz raced out of the yard to get on it.

But Sid's dog chased them. Buzz saved Woody from the dog, but then Buzz was left behind as the van pulled away! Now Woody had to help his friend.

Inside the van, Woody opened the box with the toys, got out RC, and pushed him down the van's ramp.

The other toys thought Woody was trying to get rid of RC. So they pushed Woody off the van!

The van sped away.

Buzz and Woody hopped on the speeding car. They raced to the van—and almost made it!

Unfortunately, RC's batteries died.

"Oh no!" cried Woody. "Now we'll never catch up with the van."

But then Woody got another idea. He lit the rocket that was taped to Buzz.
WHOOSH!
As RC sped towards the van's ramp, Buzz spread his wings and . . . he and Woody were flying!

42

They flew right into the car! Andy was so happy. He had thought Woody and Buzz were lost.

Buzz realized that Andy loved him. Now he knew what it meant to be a toy. It was even better than being a space hero.

All the toys were happy in Andy's new home. Soon it was Christmas. The toys were nervous. What if Andy got new and better toys?

The Green Army Men went to watch Andy and his sister open their gifts.

"Don't worry, Andy will always love you," Bo Peep told Woody, kissing his cheek.

Woody told Buzz, "We have nothing to worry about. Andy couldn't possibly get anything worse than you."

Then the Green Army Men made their report: Andy got a puppy!

UH-OH!

The End

Eye Spy

Help Sheriff Woody round up these pictures by looking back in the story.